Daddies

By Lila Prap

NORTHSOUTH BOOKS

New York / London

"It's time for bed," my Daddy said.
"Just five more minutes play."
"Then let's pretend we're animals!"
Is what he hears me say.

My daddy is a rhino,
we wallow in the swamp.
We make the whole world tremble,
when we **stomp, stomp, stomp!**

My daddy is that big giraffe,
his head high in the tree.
And when I'm feeling hungry,
he gives the best leaves all to me.

My daddy is a kangaroo,
he loves to jump around.
Together we love nothing more
than bouncing up and down.
Boing! Boing! Boing!

My daddy is a hippo,
he really loves to swim.
When we jump into the water,
nothing else fits in!

My daddy is an elephant,
he is so very strong.
But when he has to lift a tree,
he's glad that I'm along!

My daddy is a monkey
swinging through the trees.
He's a funny monkey daddy,
who loves to joke and tease!

My daddy is a snail,
and I'm a snail by birth.
We're never in a hurry—
we have all the time on Earth.

My daddy is a lion,
and when I'm by his side,
we roar as fiercely as we can,
you'll hear us far and wide.
Roooaaaaarrrrr!!!!

My daddy's a chameleon,
as quiet as can be.
Our favorite game is
hide-and-seek.
I bet he can't find me!

My daddy's a hyena,
he giggles all the time.
I love the funny jokes he tells,
'specially when they rhyme!

My daddy is a parrot,
and I'm a parrot, too.
He tells me jungle stories
when the day is through.

My daddy is an owl,
and I'm an owl, too.
At night we sing our evening tune,
who-whooo, who-whoooo,
who-whooo!

My daddy is a big brown bear,
we play all summer long.
When winter comes, we snuggle up
and wait for spring's sweet song.

Of all the Daddies in the world,
you know I love you best.
Now it's time to close our eyes.
Dad, you need some REST!